Monsters and Mist

A Fantasy Short Story Collection

by

Elizabeth Hirst

To Ann,
Thanks for stopping by the booth! Enjoy!
Much Love,
Elizabeth Hirst

Other Printed Works by Elizabeth Hirst

Novels

Flood Waters Rising (Coming July 15, 2011)

Visit Pop Seagull Publishing on the web at:

http://www.popseagullpublishing.com

Copyright 2011 by Pop Seagull Publishing
All rights reserved. No part of this book may be used or reproduced in any manner whatsoever without the written permission of Pop Seagull Publishing. For reprint permissions, please contact Elizabeth Hirst at jinyu_shanlin@yahoo.ca.

All characters in this book are fictitious. Any resemblance to persons living or dead is strictly coincidental.

Cover Design Copyright 2011 by Elizabeth Hirst
Published by
Pop Seagull Publishing
Oakville, Ontario, Canada

Printed and bound in the USA

Table Of Contents

Made of the Mist	5
Teddy Bear's Picnic	7
Ground Cover	11
Beyond Nemra	17
Mr. Oon	29

Made of the Mist

Karen breathed deeply for the first time that evening clutching the scrolled handrail along the Falls Walk. Her LED party ring picked up the cold. Behind her, cars rubbernecked along the Niagara Parkway, their drivers too befuddled by the warren of roads tunneling through the city to find a decent place to park.

Nikki led the bachelorettes like a staggering Isaac Brock. Karen thought of the painting of Brock that hung in the University foyer, in which he pointed out to the world, foot squarely planted on a dashing hunk of local sandstone, and shouted 'Surgite': press onward. Nikki leaned with one foot on a garbage can, her shot glass necklace raised to the passing traffic.

"Honk if you're horny!" She squealed, giving the beads a shake.

Nikki then dashed off down the sidewalk after a dark-complected man in a suit, sporting sparkly pink deelyboppers shaped like penises. The bachelorettes, looking like a flock of pink starlings in ballet flats, billowed around her.

Karen did not flock. Designated drivers lacked the requisite shots of Daniels to grow wings.

Nikki's laugh echoed off a stone kiosk containing a pepsi machine and a broken cement bench.

"Hey, hey sexy? Where you goin'? I love a man in uniform!" she called.

Karen rested her elbows on the rough sandstone fencing. She let the bachelorettes drift further down the parkway toward Clifton Hill while her gaze drifted over Niagara Falls. The water's constant motion traced lines across her retinas.

Damn those floodlights. Green, then blue, then red. We never really experience the Falls the way we're supposed to. I want to know the Falls that are heard but not seen. Just once, I want to feel the biting darkness of a colonial winter.

Darkness responded. Without floodlights, the Falls became a liquid mimic of the crescent moon, the mist like drifting clouds. The beat in Karen's wrist quickened against the rail until she was surprised not to hear her pulse pinging on the metal.

No traffic behind her.

An arm stretched out of the mist, then a pair of breasts attached to a torso that dissipated at the waist. A translucent white hand with fingers like river stones jointed together pushed against a rising swirl of air and water droplets. Then a gust of white spray formed a rounded face with eyes sunken into the night sky. Tendrils of long, buoyant hair blended into the hue of the icy clouds hovering over Lake Erie.

The sky eyes of the mist woman faced Karen. Karen pulled the LED ring off her right hand and wrapped it in the hem of her sweater. She checked over her shoulder for Nikki. A giant oak leaned out over the edge of the Niagara gorge where the kiosk had been, its few straggling winter leaves flipping over and back in the breeze.

Skeletons of sumach, maple and chestnut surrounded her tiny, lonely square of concrete and scrolled handrail.

The mist woman still hovered over the Falls. Karen raised her hand, waved and then closed her fingers over her palm as if grasping a delicate treasure. The mist woman raised one of her hands. Her fingertips smudged horizontally, drifting off like smoke without dissipating.

The breeze played with Karen's hair for a second too long.

"We're still here," it whispered.

"Caught you!" Nikki slurred, falling onto Karen's shoulder. The lights from the ring on Karen's finger mingled with the flood lighting trained on the Falls.

Green. Blue. Red.

Teddy Bear's Picnic

Deanie flung the bedsheets onto the floor—first the comforters, then the flat sheet. When Jack the Teddy Bear wasn't between the blankets, he reached under his mattress and pulled the fitted sheet up, too. Under Deanie's bed, a Mickey Mouse jack-in-the-box and a couple of dinky cars gathered dust. No Jack.

Deanie scanned the shelves lining his room. Stuffed animals crowded for his attention, arms outstretched, their black bead eyes saying "Forget about the bear. I'm lonely."

Some movement caught Deanie's eye, out the window. He leaned out of the open lower pane, dusk air caressing his cheek.
He closed his eyes and opened them again to be sure he wasn't still napping. Jack, his teddy bear, waddled toward the back forty on overstuffed legs. He moved quickly, but less at a run than a pattern of tottering, falling, and crawling. He reminded Deanie of a chubby kindergartener trying to avoid being 'it' at tag.

Deanie hesitated at the window before whirling around. Under his tummy he felt excitement flipping and flopping like when his Dad had told him they were going to Disney World. Still in his Cars pajamas, the red ones with Lightning McQueen and Tow Mater prancing around on them, he yanked open his closet and grabbed the necessities for a long journey: light-up cross-trainers, a Transformers lunch box filled with action figures and a yellow plastic flashlight.

He jumped into the trainers, slung the flashlight over his shoulder and swung the lunchbox in the air. "It's finally happened... the Teddy Bears' Picnic!"

Deanie clambered out the window into the apple tree. He remembered what they had taught him in first grade last year:

If you go out in the woods today,
You're sure of a big surprise. . .
Today's the day that Teddy Bears have their piiicnic!

They'd all brought their teddy bears to school. Margie from next door had a strange blue teddy bear with a Mohawk of ponytailed fur. On that day, they all sat on a big fleecy blanket from the nurse's office eating gummi bears and drinking fruit punch labeled 'Beary Juice'. The others thought that was the real Teddy Bears' Picnic.

Deanie shimmied down the apple tree and sprinted for the woodlot. Jack's chubby, waddling form edged into a yellowbell bush.

Deanie waved. "Jack! Stop, take me with you!"
Jack rustled on through the yellowbell bush, into the forest.
Deanie slowed down at the treeline. He peered into the ferns on the forest floor, shading his eyes like the re-enacted hikers on his favourite show, Outdoor Adventures. The people on Outdoor Adventures told real stories about awesome stuff like hanging off cliffs for hours before being rescued by natives and narrowly escaping maulings by various woodland creatures.

The woodland creature that Deanie sought stood over the lip of a small snow-melt ditch.

Once again, Deanie called out, "Jack, Jack!" but Jack ignored him and continued to slide down the carpet of dead leaves lining the ditch.

Deanie decided that living Teddy Bears probably couldn't hear.

As he crested the slope of the ditch, Deanie searched for the site of the picnic. All he saw was an oval patch of twilight bent across the 'v' of the ditch and a scrawny tree jutting out from one bank. There had to be a fluffy blanket somewhere, and baskets with gingham bunting filled with whatever it was Teddy Bears liked to eat.

Margie's bear with the scruffy Mohawk was there, and more bears than Deanie had met on the entire block. When they reached the twilight oval on the ditch floor, they dropped to all fours and swung their legs out when they walked, like the real bears Deanie saw on Outdoor Adventures. One bear tried to hoist itself up the trunk of a nearby tree, but kept falling backward because its arms weren't long enough and its felt body kept sticking to the bark. little tufts of red fluff stuck to the tree. Jack and another bear raised themselves up on their hind legs and battered at each other with their rounded arm stumps.

A squirrel bounded along the edge of the ditch in front of where Deanie stood. The three bears closest to it opened their terry cloth mouths. They jumped into mid-air and landed on the squirrel. A piece of fluffy tail with dark red on the tip flew out of the pile of Teddy Bears. Deanie heard a shrill scream that trailed off too quickly.

The remaining bears now stood on all fours, facing Deanie. They smiled, hideous smiles filled with unnatural teeth.

Jack sauntered up between the other bears like a confident housecat.

"Jack," Deanie pleaded, shaking his head, "We're best friends. . ."

Jack leaped out in the lead, kicking up leaves under his stub-legs as he went. Deanie screamed and ran for home, expecting every second to feel the clamping of little needle teeth around his ankles. He shot across the field, possessed of his own momentum, hurtled up three porch steps in one leap and slammed the screen door behind him. He hid under his parents' bed on the opposite side of the house.

Deanie found Jack sitting in his miniature rocking chair the next morning, slumped over the handrail. His black bead eyes seemed to say "Don't stay mad at me Deanie. It was all just a joke, right?"

Deanie poked Jack with a plastic sword. When the bear stayed still, Deanie grabbed him by one arm. Outside, the boom of distant thunder rattled the window panes.

They went back to the ditch together, Jack hanging from Deanie's arm, looking for the last time like the perfect picture of boy and best bear. Deanie stood at the edge of the ditch for a moment. He uttered a deep sigh then tossed Jack onto the dark ground in the center of the ditch.

"You're a real bear now," he said.

Ground Cover

Jenny Short liked the shiny kind of shirts that you didn't have to iron in the morning. She rolled out of bed, pulled one out of a pile on her bedroom floor with stripes on and wiggled it over her head. After staggering down to the bathroom, she stuck the deodorant stick underneath her sleeves and gave it a few quick strokes. She pulled a brush through her hair exactly five times—no more—then yanked it back into a ponytail.

A quick smile in the mirror, and she was down the steps and into the driver's seat of her automatic car, ten minutes late for work. In the early morning sunshine she noticed that her yard looked a bit. . . nicer than usual. As she pulled out of the drive, she figured out why. "When did I get a garden," she said, to no one in particular.

Old Mrs. Eglik waited for the car to pass as Jenny came up even with the sidewalk, her lips in a continual raisin shape. Jenny rolled down the window and leaned out. "Mrs. Eglik! Why do I have a garden in my yard?"

Mrs. Eglik's lips stretched from a raisin to a leathery string bean.

"If you don't know, Jenny, I'm sure I don't either."

Jenny brought Sheena home from work that night after a stop-over at McBurger's.

"See," Jenny said, wading across her weedy lawn to the little hummock slouched in the shade of her front porch, "I told you. Weird, right?"

Sheena, a short twenty-something with a button nose and glasses, finished a long pull on her strawberry milkshake.

"Maybe it's a little weird. But hey, you haven't done anything with all this space. Maybe someone else decided to do it for you."

Jenny stared at the garden. The garden stared back. Five large, round flowers on twisted stalks faced her, bending slightly in an unfelt breeze. They looked like sunflowers, with large, dark centers full of scales—what Jenny assumed to be seeds. The petals weren't quite right, though, frayed at the edges like fringe on a leather jacket. The fringe wavered in that same unfelt breeze, slowly back and forth. Below the sunflowers grew clumps of upturned hibiscus, pink and shiny as the underside of a tongue. Below them, columns of lily pushed out over the edges of the hummock on an angle. An odd shade of brown, Jenny thought that the smell in the air—the sweet, cloying smell of a high school date wearing too much cologne—came from the lilies.

Slick grey stones surrounded the whole thing: slick, although it hadn't rained in days. Sheena nudged one with her foot. It deflated, then quickly regained its shape.

Sheena drained the last of her milkshake, her eyebrows creeping up from behind her glasses as she turned to Jenny. Sheena finally broke the silence.

"Well, whoever sent you this must know you," she said with a weak little laugh, "They gave you one of those foam rocks that you can hide your extra house keys under." Jenny suggested that they go inside and listen to Jump Jet's new album. By that time, Sheena had already pulled the screen door open.

Jenny slept in late the next day. Maybe if she slept long enough, she thought, the strange garden would be gone again, as quick as it came. Finally, when the sun coming in from the windows warmed her bed so much that her blankets became a damp, smelly cocoon, she crawled to the side of her bed where the windows were and opened one. She flipped up the outside screen and leaned out of the open window. She looked down over her front porch.

Five fringed sunflowers faced up at her, swaying gently in the breeze. Out of the corner of her eye, she thought she caught one pulling its petals into the center, then releasing them—blinking?
She kept watching the garden, unsure of her own perception. The sunflowers stayed still.

A redwing blackbird glided out of the trees and grasped one of the sunflower stems in its claws. Jenny heard another bird call from across the street. The blackbird adjusted its footing and perched sideways on the stem, which now bent downward toward the cloud of hibisci. Facing the sound of the other bird, it stuck its beak out and prepared to defend its territory.

"Wha-kee," it screeched, "Wha-kee! Wha-kee!"

All the while, the hibisci drew nearer. An especially big one came in from behind, its tongue-pink, speckled petals growing slick. In a movement almost too fast for Jenny to register, the flower opened wide and snapped shut over the bird in the middle of its next cry, twisting itself with an audible crunch into the veined cone of a hibiscus bud.

Afterward, the sunflowers still stared up at her.

Jenny spent a week using the side door and checking furtively from the driver's seat of her car to see if the thing had grown. It still hadn't rained, but the garden looked slick, supple and straight of stalk. Just like her shirts and hairstyle, it seemed to require no extra care. Mrs. Eglik came knocking in the early evening the next Saturday, as Jenny placed the last of the clean dishes in her kitchen cabinet. Jenny kept her attention on the garden as much as possible as she stepped out onto the front porch with a tea towel folded over her arm. The sunflowers still watched her.

Mrs. Eglik held a basket with a pair of gardening shears in the bottom.

"Sorry to bother you, Jenny, but I couldn't help but notice those hibisci as I was on my morning constitutional. They must be very rare—I've never seen such a colour before. Do you mind if I take a cutting?"

Jenny winced inwardly.

"I'm sorry, Mrs. Eglik, but they're very delicate right now. I can't risk them wilting on me, not with this drought," she said, hoping that she sounded correct enough that the old woman would go home.

Mrs. Eglik made that string-bean frown.

"Plants are better off with less leaves in a drought. But if you don't want me to have any, I guess I'll have to live without them."

Jenny waited until Mrs. Eglik had left the yard before going back inside. She watched for an hour to make sure that she didn't come back.

Jenny, knew, in her heart, that Mrs. Eglik would eventually be back. If not Mrs. Eglik, then the dog from down the street or an unsuspecting Girl Guide. That's why, on the way home from the office on Monday afternoon, she stopped at the hardware store and picked up a bottle of weed killer. She had no proof that it would work, but the thing sure looked like flowers. Weed killer seemed as safe a bet as any. Just to hedge that bet, she also picked up a long pitchfork.

Her car rounded the corner onto Fitch Street and started passing faded townhouses. Her own townhouse was on the right, smooshed between Mrs. Eglik's and a family home with Rubbermaid-plastic cars, a half-filled wading pool and an overturned tricycle littering the yard. As she approached the driveway, she noticed a familiar folding grocery cart left at the end of her yard.

She swung into the driveway just in time to see Mrs. Eglik crouched on the ground with a hibiscus-mouth and length of stem pinched between her fingers. Jenny slammed on the brakes, but not before Mrs. Eglik opened the shears, placed them around the thick stem, and squeezed the handles.

Jenny ripped her seatbelt out of the catch and rushed from the car. A foul-smelling, pollen-like substance billowed out of the lilies. The hibisci opened to their widest, turned rug-burn red and screamed, a sound as shrill as the redwing blackbird with the slight warble of a child's plastic whistle.

Mrs. Eglik tried to back away, but the sunflowers twined around her arms and legs, pulling her toward the wet semblance of earth leaning against the front porch. The bushes parted to reveal cracked brown skin covered in coarse clumps of hair like the ones on the backs of caterpillars—an unsuspecting person would probably take the texture for mulch and cracked earth, but Jenny understood now that it was actually skin—skin and mouth. The crack widened, showing row after row of root-like digestive cilia.

Jenny yanked open the back door of her car and pulled out the weed killer and pitchfork.

"Help me, Jenny," called Mrs. Eglik, "I won't sue you, I swear!"

The garden pulled Mrs. Eglik closer. The old woman's heels made ruts in the ground as she tried to gain some traction. Jenny arrived with the weed killer. Being careful to stay out of the reach of the sunflowers, she wedged the bottle between her knees and wrenched off the cap. Jenny splashed the sunflower stalks—no withering, no squealing. She poured some more along the length of the garden, but nothing seemed to be happening, at least not fast enough to make a difference.

The dirt crack closed on the edge of Mrs. Eglik's wool skirt. The skirt gave at the elastic waistband, pooling around her ankles. Jenny picked the pitchfork up off the grass. She struck first at the inside of the mouth, jamming the tines into the wrinkly folds of brown cilia. The hibisci screamed again. Good. Jenny stuck the pitchfork in at the roots of the bushes a couple more times, with the thing making more and more grunts and squeals of displeasure. One more stab to the midsection (if such a thing had a midsection), and the whole garden mound shuddered, letting go of Mrs. Eglik. The edging stones undulated like the edges of a snail's body. Then the whole think slunk away, its movement half earthworm, half slug.

As it slithered off, sliming the next-door neighbour's tricycle, Jenny dropped the pitchfork. Mrs. Eglik took a quick survey of herself. Her control-top panty hose was candy-striped with green rubbings like grass stains. Mrs. Eglik sounded like she was about to throw up as she said, "Jenny Smith... why in the world did you have a slug disguised as a garden in your yard?"

"If you don't know, Mrs. Eglik, I'm sure I don't either," Jenny answered.

The next day, Jenny took Mrs. Eglik out shopping for a new skirt. While they were at the department store, Jenny invested in some nice cotton shirts and an iron. She bought some gas for the lawn mower and made sure there was no more clutter by the front porch.

The minister's wife a few blocks down, on Varney St., woke up that day to find a lovely new garden in her back yard. She decided to invite her friends over for sandwiches to show it off. She also decided it would look better with a birdhouse staked into it.

Beyond Nemra

Nemra squatted by the fire, the light dancing off the upturned palms of her hands. Beneath her exposed breastbone, a soft blue light flickered, making shadows of the curved bones of her ribcage.

"So," she said to Kerimar, chin upturned, "You want to know how I got this power?"

Kerimar paused a moment. "Yes, I do-- the real story this time."

"That one's costly, my Lad. Truth always comes dear." She twirled away from the fire, her arms spread out.

Kerimar watched her prance for a moment, her white skin glowing in the light of the moon. He wondered how two opposite people could end up with the same goal in life. Certainly, he had been attracted to her at first. What man and woman, facing the hardships of nature alone together are not initially drawn to each other, if only out of a need for security, stability? But Kerimar had spent much of his youth stealing cattle from rival tribes in the Downlands, and the longer he spent with Nemra, the more she reminded him of his youth. Beyond Nemra, a final few trees with light, thin bark and spade-shaped leaves stood between their
campfire and the Plain of Zephmal. Kerimar's stomach clenched, and he turned his attention back to Nemra. Plenty of time to be afraid tomorrow, when they would need that extra fear-energy to survive.

"If you don't tell the story now, you may never have another chance to tell it. Truth may be as gold, girl, but once you're gone it tarnishes quickly." He said.

The lines on Nemra's face deepened. She frowned like an old woman rather than a maiden. Her chest still glowed like a lightning bug in the heat of summer.

"All right, all right, I'll tell you what happened. There was this boy, a sorcerer's apprentice. A rather stupid fellow, all told. He had the bad fortune to fall in love with me."

A grin spread across Nemra's face that made Kerimar grateful that he had not suffered such bad fortune. Her teeth were like cat's teeth. "I warned him not to press me, but still he showed up at

my family home, and every day I had to turn him away.
Finally, I decided that maybe if I accepted his gift, he would leave me alone. Well, wouldn't you know that the stupid boy had taken one of his master's magic talismans."

Kerimar could always tell the fake tales because Nemra inevitably styled herself as the winner of every argument, the smarter of every pairing. He sighed, "So what happened then?"

"Well, naturally I asked him what it did. I said I'd only agree to take it if he told me the external, and the internal use. I think he expected me not to know about the secret internal magic of talismans, but that's silly because every little girl tells tales of talisman magic gone wrong while she's staying overnight at friends' houses. As I say, he was a stupid boy."

"So, he told you, and you swallowed it?"

"Yes. I swallowed it and skipped town. That talisman was my ticket to fortune!"

Kerimar started gathering his sleeping furs. "Or your ticket to death. There's no guarantee you can release it. I've heard of trained wizards who couldn't release an internalized talisman."

Nemra scowled. She grabbed her own sleeping fur and pulled it around herself like a piece of unleavened bread.

"Are you happy with that one? Was that a good enough story for you?" She asked with her back turned.

"A story it was, but I think that one had some truth in it. Perhaps one day you'll tell me which parts really happened."

She grunted. "Perhaps not."

* * *

Nemra's stiff-soled sandals scuffed against the dirt and pebbles marking the boundary between the forest and the Plain of Zephmal. Kerimar could see from the way that she bounced and swayed that she was restless to cross. She loosened her muscles like a runner, bending back one knee, then the other with her hand gripped around the ankle.

Nemra pulled the swords, a short and a long, out of the crossed scabbards on her back. Danno and Porda, she called them, like the lovers from the famous song. Kerimar swung his semi-circular B'rummi blade in an arc in front of him. No name could cling to this weapon, nor a scabbard contain the crescent moon-shaped blade and its wooden backing lined with handholds and sacred carvings.

"Perhaps if we clear our minds beforehand. . ." he began.

"Not from what I've heard," Nemra cut him off, "The Idol of Zephmal will see what it wants to see, no matter how hard you try to block it out."

Kerimar frowned. "I'm still going to try."

Nemra stepped toward the edge of the Plain, a rounded expanse of ankle-high grass about a mile to the center. In that center, far off, Kerimar could see a small, dark pedestal of stone with the Idol of Zephmal glittering atop it like a golden fly-candle, the kind wizards made that drew insects in only to burn them up. Kerimar tried to look stern and wise despite the fact that he was only two years Nemra's senior.

"Be careful. Once you've crossed the line for the first time..."

"Yes, yes, you can't undo the enchantment. Are we going to go anytime today? I suggest that we start at a run."

Kerimar nodded. "Yes, let's run. As soon as we finish an enemy, let's run as fast as we can. It will give them less time to multiply."

Despite their resolution, once they stepped beyond the barrier Kerimar stopped. The sky, formerly blue and filled with clusters of white clouds, instantly became a roiling purple mass of. . . well, Kerimar wasn't sure what it was, but it looked like melted wax with metal mixed into it. An ambient, lazy sort of light floated in the air in place of the sun. He saw Nemra in his peripheral vision, paused in the same manner. He forced himself to push onward, keeping his eyes on the dark pedestal in the center of the plain.

By the time Kerimar had reached a jog, Nemra tilted ahead at an all-out run. He could see her bounding ahead of him like an antelope fleeing a savannah cat, her swords held aloft as deadly horns. Long brown hair, brown as Kerimar's skin in the heat of summer, streamed out behind her in a half-gathered ponytail. She was a thin girl, with a flat, boyish bottom and a chest to match. Kerimar couldn't imagine the round-hipped, supple women of the B'rummi clan having much luck running the way Nemra did. No, Nemra was well fitted for battle, but Kerimar often wondered if she had always seen battle as her only end.

Kerimar noticed the bulb of faint green light growing from the base of Zephmal's pedestal as soon as it appeared, but it had turned to a dome and swept over them both before he could cry out a warning to Nemra. She was still a little ahead of him, lunging into the plain and uttering a shrill battlecry.

Once the dome swept over them a beast was there, directly in Nemra's path. Kerimar grimaced at the giant creature, a monstrous bull with hooves girded in iron and blank, pus-coloured eyes rolling in its head. Its hooves, even considering its size, were twice the proportion of a normal animal. It bellowed and charged at Nemra, who continued to run with unflinching ease. Kerimar ran to the place where they must meet, eager to pull her to safety—silly girl, why did he have to throw in his lot with someone with a death wish? Talisman or no talisman, she should. . .

Kerimar got close to Nemra and the bull, but not close enough. Nemra met the monster head-on and, using its giant horns for leverage (each horn easily the size of one of her legs) she vaulted over its head, legs spread, and landed on its back, where she eagerly thrust her two swords through its spine. The bull bellowed as its legs seized up beneath it, not so much slowing to a stop as skidding into the ground. Nemra jumped off of the bull's back before it could roll over on her and stood with her hands on her knees and her back to the fiend, panting. Her long sword, Danno, protruded from the bull's ribcage.

Kerimar noticed that the beast was still breathing. With a quick arc of his B'rummi blade, he severed its head most of the way across. Dark purple sludge like the swirling mess in the sky ran down the edge of the blade.

He leveraged his own weight against the carcass of the beast to dislodge Nemra's sword. It came out with a sound like a bare foot sliding through rotten pumpkin. With one hand, he held it out to Nemra, blade down so as to let it drip.

"Next time, let me in on the fight," he said.

"Next time, run a little faster," she replied, and then, taking the sword, "What was that thing, anyway? I might've been sick on rancid beef once or twice, but that's not quite the same thing."

They took off at a jog. Kerimar contemplated answering her—after all, hadn't she just been lying to him the whole way about her past? But his tribe had a saying: silence breeds deceit.

"I stole my fair share of steers on the Downlands as a child. One of my earliest nightmares is of being trampled in a stampede."

"Ah," she said, tenuous and quick. Kerimar frowned. That tone of voice, that uncertain expression had haunted him for most of his life, in barrooms when people recognized his weapon, in guards' huts when some city dweller decided he looked suspicious just for existing. Without an overt question, still he answered, "The B'rummi used to live off the land, before the Lords put farms and estates on it. Now all of our hunting grounds, which fed hundreds of people, are fenced off for the use of very few. They tax us like any other citizens, but we're not the same as other citizens. We don't make a lot of things that the Lords want to buy. Except people, of course."

"But if you could barter your land back from the Lords, if you had enough money..."

Kerimar nodded once, forcefully. "The Idol of Zephmal is worth almost anything to Lord Rilch."

Nemra's severe nose flared a little at the edges, the hard lines along her eyes softened. "I... I can respect that."

As they talked, Zephmal's pedestal clarified in the distance from a blurry black shoot pushing out of the ground to a small tree of black stone supporting a terrible, golden oval fruit. The green light rose up like a bubble in boiling soup then burst over them again.

This time, when the light passed, a group of humanoid figures formed a wide ring around them. Kerimar saw that they were shabbily dressed in old homespun frocks and heavy cotton overalls, some of them with punctured straw hats wobbling above their brows. He counted about thirty, in all, before a wild-eyed peasant woman with a pitchfork coated in pig shit thrust her weapon toward his heart. He parried the blow with his crescent blade, grimaced, and backed toward Nemra. He could kill this woman quickly, but—a peasant? He hesitated.

The old woman leaned forward, sticking her weatherworn chin out so far that Kerimar could see several hairs growing off the end.

"Ehhh, you brazen young quean, what think ye now of breakin' your love vow?" the old woman dribbled out in a beat-driven regional patois. Kerimar doubted instantly that this was any fear of his. Peasants might have often mistrusted him, but he had never felt any fear of them, especially not in the presence of his B'rummi blade. He felt his back touch Nemra's, and suddenly he could feel her parrying other peasants behind him. More enemies drifted in behind the old woman, and from all sides—Kerimar would have to do something, and quickly.

"Kill her, Kerimar!" Nemra urged from behind him.

The old woman gave a nudge on the pitchfork. Her strength grew with Kerimar's misgivings.

"They're just peasants, Nemra."

"No, they're sludge replicas of peasants taken out of our brains. Get slicing!"

Kerimar gritted his teeth while he thrust the old woman back, pitchfork and all, then lunged forward and sliced her across the midsection. She bled out purple sludge from the slash in her frock like a river breaking its dam, until she had melted into a half-formed pile of skin and limbs. Kerimar slashed and parried with all his might after that, deftly dodging blows from post hammers, swipes with meat cleavers. One particularly spirited peasant managed to smack his arm with a board and nail before losing his head, but before long Kerimar and Nemra stood within a circle of half-melted bodies, their sandals coated in purple grime.

Kerimar took a strip of linen out of his pack and tied it around his punctured arm. He looked at Nemra, who was leaned over again, hands on her knees. The blue glow inside her chest flickered like a candle covered with moths. Normally, it pulsated gently with the beat of her heart.

"Nemra, are you all right?"

She didn't answer.

"Nemra?"

She groaned like someone who had been sick to their stomach—fifteen times.

"That one was me," she said.

Kerimar went to her and pushed up on her shoulders, straightening her. He looked into her angular face and tried to catch her shifting brown eyes with his. She struggled at first, but eventually looked him in the eyes.

He had never observed her eyes before, never been allowed to look at them for more than a few seconds as she chided him for burning the beans or insisted for the thousandth time that she had no secrets. Now, with her face sheened in sweat and the talisman in her chest beating its light against her like a bird against a cage, her eyes opened before him, deep brown roses so dark that the iris was barely distinguishable from the pupil. She trembled.

"The Old Woman spoke of a love vow," Kerimar said gently.

"Stop looking at me like that!" Nemra wrenched herself away from him, "Stop looking!"

Nemra froze for a moment with her swords raised. Kerimar kept his blade at his side.

"I wonder how long you will try to protect that which is destroying you."

Nemra bolted ahead, leaving Kerimar the difficult task of catching up again. This time, however, he pushed himself to stay with her. The enemies were multiplying with every encounter, and if his assumptions were correct, the next one would be even more dangerous. She would need him by her side, whether she wanted him there or not.

Zephmal's pedestal, now stable at the size of a temple pillar, with stairs running in a spiral up its side shot out another green missive. It washed over them both. When the light-blindness cleared away a small army stood before them clad in familiar livery. Lord Rilch, a short, squat man with a ring of salt-and-pepper hair stood at the front of a host of sixty armed disciples of Zephmal. Kerimar stopped, Nemra beside him.

"This fear is mine," he said.

"No, it's mine," she replied. The light in her chest strobed until the flesh above looked entirely translucent, ready to
disappear into the next world. Rilch's fur-lined robes, the same hue as the green light emanating from the idol, brushed the ground

he pointed them out to the troops.

"There they are, the traitors! They will die for forsaking the idol! Take them, in the name of Zephmal!"

The disciples, also clad in light green tabards and tunics, raised their spears and let out a mighty roar. They swarmed around Rilch as a river around a rock, and soon Kerimar and Nemra faced a solid line of them, their spears outstretched. Rilch remained behind, yelling the same sort of religious zealotry as before.

Kerimar yelled to Nemra over the shouts of the oncoming soldiers. "Release the talisman! Now!"

Nemra held out her swords, but her arms bent a little too much, quivered a little too fiercely.

"I can't," she said, and Kerimar knew from the deathly stretch of her lips over her exposed teeth that she told the truth. Finally, at this late hour, she was telling the truth about something.

In the end, with no other choice, they met the spearmen.

Kerimar dodged three of the spears directly in front of him, swinging his arm down with the B'rummi blade to cut them in half as they passed. Another spear, this one behind him, caught him in the fleshy part of his side. He swung his weapon and cut the spear off at the shaft before its wielder could drive it deeper toward his vital organs. Over and over again he swung his blade around him in a wide arc, sometimes connecting with weapons and more often connecting with purple-spurting flesh. All around him spearmen melted, but still more pressed in to replace them. Nemra, at first, was lost in the crowd, but then she was beside him, fleeing three disciples. The right side of her face ran slick with blood. It looked to Kerimar as though her ear had been maimed while ducking a spear.

Kerimar estimated when Nemra came running to him that they had killed thirty or so of the original sixty spearmen, but still thirty or more pressed toward them as they fought. Kerimar slashed through the chest of one spearman, and as the spearman disintegrated he made a path for them to flee toward the idol.

Nemra pointed at Rilch, who still stood perhaps a hundred feet from the base of the pedestal yelling insults.

"He's the main fear. Maybe if we kill him, the others will disintegrate."

Kerimar nodded, but his chest did not permit him to bring in a large enough breath to speak a sentence, not while he had to run. The pain in his side turned into a cramp which caused him to stop for a moment.

Nemra stopped, looked back. Kerimar waved her on. The spearmen swarmed around him, and he forced himself to move his arms, swinging his blade in an unconscious exchange of blow and counterblow. Several of the spearmen collapsed into gelatin under his weapon's edge, but still more crowded in on him. One large disciple in particular gained on him even as he parried the blows of others. With a deranged bellow of triumph he raised his spear and plunged downward. Kerimar steadied himself for the final blow.

Only the squelch of disintegrating ooze accosted him. Rilch's voice left the plain, and so did the sounds of the other soldiers. He opened his flinching eyes to discover the soldiers around him melting into the earth with the same rotten-pumpkin squish as the others they had vanquished.

Nemra held Danno up over what was left of Rilch's prone body.

"We've made it!" she called.

Kerimar limped to where she was, the pain in his side flaring with every step. When he reached her, he pushed her swords aside and caught Nemra up in a tight embrace. She tensed at first, but then relaxed and allowed his chin to sink into her hair. The smell of battle was in that hair, blood and sweat, the smell of courage. And yet, Kerimar thought he understood now what she was hiding. The final lie he had been unable to solve had come undone in Rilch's appearance here.

"I don't think that Rilch came here because of either one of us," he said, "I think he came here because of both of us."

Nemra scowled up at him. "So?"

Kerimar let her go and walked on in his slow, limping gait toward the pedestal.

"So, if Rilch didn't have anything you want, you wouldn't be afraid to disappoint him. All along the journey here, you would have me believe that you only came to the plain for the thrill of battle."

She followed him, with the posture of a heckler following a

condemned criminal. "You still don't know why I want the reward."

Kerimar grinned. . . even his grin grew laboured with the wound in his side. "I know your secret, girl. For your sake I'll keep it to myself."

As they closed the rest of the distance to the pedestal, Nemra walked alongside him, fidgeting and twisting and sometimes opening her mouth to say something to him, but ultimately remaining silent until they reached the first few steps at the base. When she opened her mouth and when she showed her teeth, Kerimar saw blue talisman light spilling out. Her chest glowed totally blue now, the talisman casting her ribcage into stark silhouette as though her heart was a pulsating piece of some foreign sun.

She held her arm out to Kerimar, helping him up each stair carefully and deliberately. In spite of himself, he felt goosebumps spread up his skin when she touched him with those long, ivory-white hands of hers. Despite the fact that she helped him, her face was taut with emotion. Her shoulders also depicted a tension not derived from clinging to his arm.

"If you know what happened to me, you have to tell me," she quavered.

Kerimar hoisted himself up another painful step. Five steps from the top, he felt his strength flagging. The world swam around him. He put his other hand on Nemra's arm. "I can't go any further."

Her fingers dug into his forearm. "Tell me then I'll let you rest."

"I knew as soon as the old woman mentioned the love vow," Kerimar said, "You didn't steal the talisman. You had a lover. He gave it to you as a sign of your betrothal, and you broke faith and left him for fame and fortune."

She barked out a laugh, a dry cough almost. "Is that really all you think of me after I saved your life?" Nemra bent her knees and collapsed against the round wall of the pedestal. She slung a hand over one knee and leaned forward. She bore her glowing blue teeth when she talked.

"I may have left, but it was he who wronged me. After the betrothal, it was as though he didn't see me anymore. He was lost in his studies, in other people outside of our home. A thousand times my friends would tell me about something he said or did that he never mentioned to me. My love had proved himself incapable of ever loving me. I swallowed the stone with a vow to make enough money to live independently forever, or die trying. I didn't expect you to understand."

Kerimar watched her, trembling there on the step. The outline of Nemra's jawbone now stood out from the blue glow creeping up her throat. She croaked out one final statement as she got up to finish the steps, "But as you said, there are trained wizards who can't release an internalized talisman."

Nemra almost crawled up the steps, her posture stooped and her hands out in front of her as if she would fall at any moment.

Kerimar called after her. "I understand now, Nemra. I'm sorry. . ." But Nemra didn't answer. The idol lay before her, an oval carving of gold depicting Zephmal, the monkey-god of riches and business. His flipper hands held the likeness of a city-state coin. Nemra put a hand on either side of the statue and lifted it.

A disc of pale green light shot out of the pedestal to the margins of the plain. In the wake of that light, the plains writhed with newly awakened life. Kerimar suspected the life out there was more like life newly awakened from the dead. The faces were all the same, thin, human and blonde. A horde of the same man covered the plain, each with a slightly different injury and milky, filmed-over eyes. The multiple 'he' wore an apprentice wizard's robe, white alchemist's pants and rural-looking boots. They groaned, they screeched, and all of them hurled themselves headlong at the pillar.

Nemra dropped the idol. It rolled across the pedestal top with a hollow clang.

"Kerimar, no! It's him!"

The undead betrotheds (for Kerimar was certain now that's what they were) surged up the stairs with an unusual speed, knocking each other off of the rail-less steps in their eagerness to get to the top.

Kerimar cried out, "Release the talisman! For both of our lives, you have to release it!" One betrothed reached Kerimar before the rest—he summoned enough strength to kick it. It lost balance and fell into two or three more undead men crowding toward him.

"No, I won't let you hurt him!" Nemra cried to the fiends surging up the stairs, and to the rest of the plain of undead.

It was then that Kerimar reached out for Nemra, but Nemra wasn't there anymore. Her eyes were gone, and in their place was the piercing blue glow of the talisman. For a moment she stood there as though she were only standing because a fine piece of thread held her up from the tip of her head. That moment ended when she thrust her arms out to the sides and her chin to the sky. Her chest heaved, expanded, heaved again.

Finally she coughed, and that cough became a roar, and blue fire surged out of her mouth and into the purple malaise of the sky. The swirling masses there froze in their churnings, turning grey in a wave rippling outward from where Nemra's flame had pierced them.

Another undead betrothed staggered toward Kerimar, swinging its clawed hands in his direction. In an instant its chest was pierced through by what Kerimar at first thought was a ray of light from the sky. As the man disintegrated before him, Kerimar saw that it was actually a coal, about the size of his fist, flaming and bright blue. More coals rained down from the heavens, striking the undead minions of the plain of Zephmal with deadly accuracy. From the pedestal to the outer reaches of the plain where they had entered, the men collapsed and pooled together in a sea of sludge.

Kerimar pulled himself up the remaining few stairs to the top of the pedestal. There, as the flaming hail petered out as naturally as a real rainstorm, he crawled over to Nemra.

She lay on her side, breathing slowly in and out. Kerimar watched the swell of her bosom, free of the sickly blue glow and longed to touch her. Lying there on the black stone, she breathed deeper and easier than Kerimar had ever seen her do. She was softer now somehow, freer.

Her eyes opened as Kerimar leaned over her, the black ropes of his hair touching her sweet skin. Her lips parted, and she whispered, "I think I may love yet."

Mr. Oon

Genya reached out her hand and touched the sky. Its cold, wet surface rippled for a moment, then broke and dribbled down her arm. A shadow passed over the group of pilgrims that she had climbed the sky scaffold with, and she saw that it was a great whale. A shoal of fish fluttered by at close range. A little girl of about three tugged at her mother's robes and pointed at the many-coloured creatures that swam around above them. What a beautiful day for a child's first climb.

Genya studied the others around her and realized that she was the only one in her group that wasn't totally fixated on the surface of the sky, its flawless, calm texture and its turquoise hue. None of them were looking at the Sunfish. Granted, they could see the Sunfish from home, but Genya wanted to see it up close. She squinted into the depths to catch the luminescence of its underbelly peeking out from behind a school of carp. It swished its tail back and forth, back and forth, making no effort to get anywhere fast. The Sunfish would round the horizon in the next twenty-four hours or so, just as it had for all of memorable time.

The pyres that rounded the observation platform at the top of the sky scaffold caused most of the pilgrims to let down their hoods despite the moisture in the air. Genya had been on several pilgrimages, but she had never seen the sky so clearly until the scaffold authority decided to start the pyres. The fishes sparkled more brilliantly in fire light, and even on the stormiest days it became easier to peer into the depths where the most interesting sky creatures lurked. The pyre in the middle of the platform burned the most brightly. A pyramid of logs the size of two men, it illumined the heavens for all to see.

A hiss resounded over the platform. The main pyre smoked and sputtered. The scaffold guards, who each manned a corner of the platform scowled. One of them with more badges on his jacket than the rest strode over.

"Well, what's all this about? That only usually happens when it rains."

Another two drops made the pyre protest, and then a small trickle began to come down constantly from a point just above where the smoke met the sky. Half of the fire went out. Genya had never seen anything like it before. She backed away from her place near the middle of the observation deck, heading for the stairs.

At the top of the staircase, she paused. She told herself that she was being silly. The sky didn't change. She forced herself to watch as the bewildered guard stretched out a hand, letting the trickle wet his glove. After a moment, he smiled.

"Carry on folks, no need for alarm. It must be some kind of isolated shower."

A crack rang out over the platform like the shattering of a great stone wall. A powerful wind gusted out from the hole in the heavens that sent Genya tumbling down the platform stairs and into a railing. She threw her arms around a support beam and clung there, wind and water spray whipping at her clothes. Water poured from the sky through a hole as wide around as a small whale. It fanned out somewhat as it fell, but that did not prevent it from exerting force on those underneath. The guard that had been investigating the hole slipped backward along the observation deck. He scrabbled to gain a hand hold on the wooden planks, but the torrent swept him over the edge of the scaffolding. He fell, flailing and screaming to the ground far below. Some of the other pilgrims made it to the stairways at either side of the platform, but others were swept to the edge. They clung there, hollering for help. Genya swung from rail to rail down the rest of the platform stairs and took shelter under the next level of scaffolding. She and a few others moved to the edges and pulled the dangling, terrified people in from the top.

No sooner had Genya pulled the last panicked boy from the edge of the deck than she heard a groan from the wood of the sky scaffold. Boards overhead cracked and foaming water gushed through. She ran to the staircase with the guards and beckoned for the others to follow.

"Get off the platform," she yelled, "The top's going to collapse!"

Pilgrims tripped over their robes in tens as they stumbled down the stairs to the next level. Genya urged them on with flailing arms, watching more boards crack and more white water burst through. When everyone was safely on their way, she followed them down the stairs. She heard the platform collapse a moment later, accompanied by a foaming wave that arced over the sides of the sky scaffold. Genya concentrated on keeping pace with those in front of her and kept descending, always descending to the ground and safety.

* * *

The rain from the hole in the sky hadn't stopped after two days. Around noon that day, starfish and other small creatures started falling to earth with the rain. A sea urchin smacking against the diamond-paned window of the Bull and Breeches Inn caused Genya to bite her cheek.

The Father, with all of his faithful pilgrims behind him moved forward to embrace her. She opened her arms to him and relished the gentle prickle of his woolen robe. His Sunfish pendant left an indented feeling on her ribcage long after he let go.

"Farewell, Father. I'm sorry that I can't return home with you just yet. These people will need carpenters to help rebuild the sky scaffold." Genya said.

The wrinkles around the Father's eyes and mouth grew deeper. "I don't advise this, Genya. Why not come home with us first, and then come back once the crisis is over? The townsfolk say that if this storm keeps up, flooding will render the valley impassable in a few days." He gestured to the open door, and beyond. Merdona sloped down the mountain, away from the inn which was near the peak and the sky scaffold. At the bottom of the hill, what had been a lush green ring of valley now pooled with water. In a few days, if the rain did not stop, it would become a lake. She put her hands over the Father's. Their hands were similarly gnarled, despite the difference in ages. Most of her knuckles had scars on them, and her right middle fingernail was warped from the time that she almost sawed it right off.

"I'll be fine," she said, "The Merdona Mountain Mayor has assured me that it's just a summer storm. They're offering me a year's wages to stay for a few days of work. With that amount of money,

The Father frowned. "Just take care of yourself, child. May you always have the Sunfish in your sights."

Genya nodded, and repeated the common farewell. The Father moved to the head of the group, and they filed out the door on their way out of town. She watched them from the porch as they made their way down the main road, and stayed there even after they had turned a corner and moved out of sight.

Some time later, a bass flopped at her feet.

* * *

A week into the rainstorm, Genya turned the last page of the last book she could afford with her pilgrimage money and found out, in the inevitable yet surprising fashion of narrative, that the wizard had indeed done it. Guppies bounced off of every window of the inn as well as the roof, making a steady white noise that reminded her of small bread rolls hitting a barn door. Every once in a while she could hear a large smack coming from above. Those were the bass. Luckily, the sea urchins had subsided after a day or so. The inn's tavern was full of bedraggled messengers during those first days, begging whiskey for their friends who had been at the receiving end of a plummeting urchin.

Her stomach gurgled louder than the bread roll thumps so she knew it was time to go outside. Over in the corner of her room leaned a contraption that some of the local craftsmen were selling to help people get on with their everyday business. Made of stacked wooden crates, the body cage had arm and leg holes to allow for freedom of movement. They kept the fishes from hitting you in the face, but heaven help you if you got knocked down. Or if you were too fat to fit in the crates.

Genya lifted the body cage up, careful not to bump it against the ceiling. Once she had fitted herself into the middle like the stick of a butter churn, she poked her arms out of the sides and was ready to go. Grabbing a basket from the bed, she headed out through the tavern and into the murky daylight.

Once she was away from the porch, the guppies assaulted her. The rain was heavy, but at least she was used to rain. Fins smacked against her arms; little toothless mouths pinched her as they struggled to find purchase on her skin. Inside the crate suit she swerved back and forth, guided by the currents of the winds and the solid smack- smack- smack of fish. A bass struck the top of her cage and shoved the contraption down onto her shoulders. Genya rubbed them, hoping they wouldn't bruise.

Once she was far enough away from the overhang of the inn, she placed the open basket near some others that were rapidly filling with fish. Genya had never tasted fish before the beginning of the downpour. In the entire world, there were only a few places where the water was wide enough and deep enough to have a lot of fish. The Father said that they were food from heaven, reserved only for the very rich or the very holy. It was hard to feel holy, she thought, when you wore a box with arm holes and guppies smacked you from all sides.

Thunder rippled outward from the top of the sky scaffold. A great shape loomed above the hole, a shadow with fins and a sizeable tail. Genya put her hands out in front of her and realized that the rain was slowing down. Inside the inn, other patrons gathered by the windows to see what was blocking out the sunfish.

A huge, white nose protruded from the hole. Close behind its smooth, upturned mouth, the creature had two beady black eyes, disproportionate to the rest of its face. The sky roiled around it. Rings of waves pushed inward and crashed against its face, making it squirm and call out.

"Ooooooooon," it said. Nobody had ever heard the call of a heavenly creature before. Genya crouched down and drew her arms into her crate armor, sure that she would be deafened, or worse. When the creature called out again she could still hear it. On shaking knees, she drew back into the relative safety of the inn porch.

The creature slipped slowly out of the hole. Wave upon wave crashed against it, pushing it further toward the long drop to earth. Genya could identify it now as a small whale. It shook against the waves, writhing, flipping its fins and making that same, resonating call. The water burst forth again, turning the whale end over end down the mountain at enormous speed. She scampered inside before the impact, hoping that the inn was sturdy enough to shelter them all.

Inside, she heard the rain attack the windows with renewed vigor. She ran to the nearest one to see a blurry outline of the whale tumble the final few feet into the valley. Would the accumulated flood water be enough to break its fall? She winced. A mother beside Genya covered the eyes of her little boy.

The whale landed on its side, curled into the shape of a ring of dough with a bite out of it. A wall of white water rose up to cover it. Windows broke in the houses near the impact zone, sending shards of glass confetti out into the street. A tongue of debris-filled flood water slid up toward the inn. On its tip rode a garden gate and a grey goose with its neck twisted round. It lapped at the base of the sunfish statue in the town square. Then, with a sickly sucking sound, it drew back into the confines of the lake. Innumerable small crates, shingles, loose boards and shop signs went with it.

Genya turned away from the window for a moment. She could feel the deep tan colour seeping away from her cheeks. Around her, people scrambled about, avoiding the windows that they had been transfixed to just a moment earlier. The mother and her little boy rushed into the arms of a tall man, and both began to sob. Some youths were clustered in a tight ring of worried postures by the bar, twittering and gesticulating. No one bothered to wait and see what would happen to the whale.

She turned back to the window and scanned the lake. The peaked roofs of flooded houses spattered its surface for a few hundred feet. The debris from the wave also gathered at the edge, making the water look solid enough to walk on. Beyond that, a white hump bobbed up and down. Looking closer, Genya could see that the hump had a flipper. She bit her lip. No other signs of motion stirred the water.

Someone placed a meaty hand on her shoulder. The man was twice as tall as her, and covered in dark brown hair.

"What a shame," he said.

The other inn patrons carried on around them, gossiping and crying and taking inventory of their possessions.

Genya said, "It looks as though we're the only ones who cared about the whale. The heavens are falling around us, and all anyone

anyone can talk about is how their homes are getting soaked."

The man raised an eyebrow, a half grin curling his lips. His left hand slid off of her shoulder. He offered her his right.

"I'm Jaken, the blacksmith," he smiled, "but my friends call me Ox."

She pulled her thick black hair behind one ear, and accepted his handshake. "I'm Genya."

Ox didn't let go of her hand. Instead, he clapped another one on top. Genya tensed, but stopped herself from pulling away.

"That's the craftsmen's greeting!" She trembled. He dropped her hands. A touch of pink stole into his already ruddy cheeks.

"You're a carpenter, aren't you? Why shouldn't I greet you that way? I was sent here by some of the members of the craftsmen's guild. We heard there was a lady carpenter staying at the Bull and Breeches."

Genya sighed, and made sure it was loud enough that Ox could hear.

"Go ahead," she said as she put her arms out and turned around slowly, "Take a good look at me. I can haul out my certification papers if you want, just to complete the spectacle."

She completed the circle. Ox's face deepened into a dissatisfying, all-over red.

"Excuse me, Miss Genya, but I'm not sure that you understand me correctly. I'm not some sort of. . . gawker. I just assumed that lady carpenters were more common in other parts, is all."

Genya let her hair fall back over her face. "No," she sighed, "Sorry for the misconception."

Silence crept in between them. They both turned woodenly to the window. She didn't look at anything in particular, until a deep bass voice drew her attention back to the lake.

"Ooooooon," it called, "Ooooooon."

She gripped the windowsill to peer better through the rain. The whale's white hump wiggled, struggled along just under the chop. Its nose surfaced. Underneath, the mouth hung open, displaying a row of off-white nubs. It swam, listing to the left, until it reached the submerged roof of Merdona's other inn. There the whale rested with its red mouth turned to the sky. Its left fin, now visible

visible above the water, bent at a ninety degree angle in the middle. The whale swallowed some falling bass and hooted to itself. Genya turned to Ox because he was the only one near.

"He made it. He might be injured but he made it just the same." She said with a half-smile.

Ox crossed his arms and said, "I'd say he's got quite a good thing going here. He won't even have to work to get his food. I had a feeling that we shouldn't underestimate a beast from heaven."

Genya let her brow relax. "What was it that you came here to tell me?"

"We're having a meeting," he answered, "to see what's to be done about this leak in the sky. Tomorrow night, at the Guild Hall in the center of town."

She smiled. "And I assume that I'm invited?"

Ox leaned toward her. He looked both ways, before saying, "Maybe. How do you feel about the sky scaffold?"

Genya puzzled. "I loved seeing the sky up there, if that's what you mean. The sunfish fascinates me . . . but I'm sure you've seen it up close. With the torches burning, you could see a lot more of the creatures. It was amazing until the water started coming down. Hopefully after the rain stops, my team can make the scaffold beautiful again," she said.

She could smell the porridge on his breath when he sighed and said, "I thought so. Did you happen to think of why the mayor might want to hire a foreigner over one of Merdona's own craftsmen, and an inexperienced foreigner at that?"

"No . . ."

He frowned. "It's because none of our own will do it. We don't want the scaffold to go up again and especially not with those awful torches. Haven't you ever seen what happens when a pot of water sits over a fire for too long? The water disappears. It's the same with the sky. We made the torches too big and something evaporated. If we don't tear the scaffold down, this will just keep happening."

Genya drew back from Ox. "So you're saying that if I give up my job working on the sky scaffold, you'll let me come to your meeting," she asked, crossing her arms.

He reddened and rubbed his arms. The hair crackled under

his touch. "Well, we'd want to know that you had the same goals, at least," he mumbled.

"I do," she frowned. "I want to save Merdona from this flooding, but I need the money from the scaffold repairs to build my own store. The crafts guild in my town won't let me manage the one that I inherited from my father. I can't give up this job or it could take me another ten years to save up enough money."

"Oh," Ox said, "I'm sorry to hear that. I guess I'll be on my way then, Miss Genya. I've got other places to visit today." He moved to the door, grabbed his cloak and pulled the door to.

Genya clenched her fists. Not even a parting craftsmen's handshake!

"Excuse me," she said, striding after him, "but I think you've made a mistake! This is an emergency. There are large sky creatures falling on us. The town is going to be totally flooded in a few days. You're going to refuse my help because you want to quibble about politics? That's stupid. I'm showing up anyway."

A carp flopped through the doorway, splashing water onto Genya's leggings. Ox picked the little fish up and tossed it over his shoulder.

"Try it," he said, jutting out his chin. "I'm the guild master. You won't get far."

Ox turned his back on her. Too big to wear a crate suit, he cleared the front porch wearing only a woolen double-breasted shell. Fishes smacked against his bare head and shoulders, but he kept on walking with his back straight. Genya opened her mouth to say something. Nothing came out.

* * *

The lanterns along the main street of Merdona kept everything lit in a hazy orange glow, but the rain kept the light from reaching very far. Genya crept through the shadows near the alleyways, always glancing twice about her before making any move into the street.

She reached the millinery shop two buildings away from the guild hall and paused, her hands gripping the peeled wood siding. A crash resounded from the last alley she had been in . . . another tuna. Tunas fell from the sky in schools now- people stayed inside wondering when the next storm would be. Genya estimated that the bulk of the school would start coming down in about twenty minutes.

Under the eaves, she had a better view of the road than those on the road would have of her. With night closing in and the threat of another tuna storm on the way, people chose to move quickly toward the guild hall, huddled together in large groups. The ones wearing crate suits clacked together like wooden spoons. She waited for a particularly large, boisterous party to pass by and then slipped out of the alley. Trailing along behind them, she listened. A man with an expensive looking leather cloak led the group. Genya remembered the mayor's voice from the meeting when he hired her.

"It behooves me to attend this meeting, although I assure you that all of this planning will come to nothing. The rain is reaching its worst point as we speak; it will peter out after this. Then we can fix the sky scaffold and the guilds will look very silly indeed," he scoffed, eliciting a series of cultured giggles.

The lapping sound of waves a few hundred feet away caused Genya to doubt the mayor's optimism. In the dark the rainwater lake rippled uneasily, sprays passing over it like shadowed wings. For a moment, she allowed herself to picture the town a few days in the future. The rain could easily cover the guild hall -and all of Merdona proper- in that amount of time.

She huddled as close to the mayor's party as she could without touching anyone. When they reached the door, a well-dressed balding man let them in. Genya guessed that he was a tailor. She pulled her hood close about her face and waited for him to say something. He only scowled, pulled the door to the guild hall wider, and let them pass. The mayor waded into a tangle of people who crowded toward him. As he struggled to remove his wet outer garments, he elbowed townsfolk out of the way. Genya remarked to herself that the charisma of the mayor lay in the fact she could not tell whether he elbowed them intentionally or by necessity. People's voices rose above the general chatter in the room.

"Mr. Mayor, why haven't you let anyone near the scaffold?"

"Mr. Mayor, what do you plan to do about the flooding?"

The people crowded inward around the mayor, stretching out their hands. While a tornado of bodies swirled around him, Genya used the distraction to edge inside the room and into a dark corner at the back. Several tall men stood between her and the speaker's podium. With any luck, no one would notice her there. She kept her cape on just to be sure.

With as little movement as possible, she scanned the room for Ox. Men and women packed themselves in everywhere, and still more people entered. Spectators even lined the small loft staircase at the back, elbowing each other for a better foothold. Ox stood out from all the others. He brooded behind the podium, his dark, bushy brows casting his eyes into obscurity in the orange torch light. When the mayor and his various hangers-on drifted over to one side of the room and remained there, Ox's gaze followed them. Frowning deeply, he pushed out of his chair.

"Order, order," Ox called, stomping his foot on the raised wooden platform. The crowd's chatter dulled to a shapeless muttering. Ox stomped a few more times and the room became quiet. A small trickle of sound issued from the place where the mayor sat with his aides, but Ox seemed satisfied. He straightened a little, allowed his lips to curl up into a half smile and placed his hands on the podium.

He leaned a little toward the crowd and said, "Alright, you all know why we're here tonight. We've got to come up with a way to save Merdona. I've spent all of my assets just keeping the guildsmen out of harm's way and organizing this meeting, so I don't have time to be thinking up any fancy plans. Some of you, on the other hand, have had plenty of time to think of something, especially those of you who came from the bottom of the hill. That's why I'm going to open up the floor. Let's keep things orderly, now. You know I can take you all on if I have to."

Ox flexed his hairy biceps, and the crowd erupted in laughter. Faceless people started to call out ideas.

"Let's build one of them boats out of the wreckage," called a tenor voice, "I seen the ones they got by the sacred lake in Belzoa. If we built a big enough boat, we could all sail to safety!"

A woman's voice answered, "Yeah, Eustace, but if the leak in the sky don't stop, the whole world will be flooded eventually. Then what'll we do, live on the boat for the rest of our lives?"

Ox rubbed his beard. "That's a good start, though, Eustace. Let's have another one." He said.

This time, the unmistakable sound of the mayor's voice echoed through the hall. "I say that we wait out this storm and in the mean time, we kill that blasted whale and hand out his meat to the dispossessed homeowners as recompense for their damages. Think of the tallow that all of his fat could make! We'd be the city of a thousand torches!"

"Torches are what got us into this mess, you shortsighted nit!" Someone yelled. The room shook with boo's.

Genya hugged herself, suddenly chill. At least the townsfolk didn't mean the whale any harm. If anything, killing a heavenly creature would bring more sky-holes down on them all. She fingered her sunfish medallion. People pressed in on the mayor again. He stood up taller and tried to lean away from them. Ox waved his arms, refusing to let the crowd lose focus.

"Hey, hey, hey," he hollered, "let's not wander off topic now. That was a bad idea, but there must be more people with plans than just those two. Who's got more?"

A woman's voice called out this time. She was only a few feet away from Genya, an old matron with breasts and hips that bulged out from the ties of her apron.

"We should clean up all this danged wreckage, form it into a ball with some nails and rope, and use that to plug up the hole. Our carpenters can build a winch big enough! I seen them haul whole caravans worth of goods up the sheer side of this mountain with their contraptions."

The crowd murmured with excitement. Genya, in her darkened corner, felt her mind stir with the ideas the villagers put forward. The old woman's idea had merit, but there were several problems with it. First of all, with all of the debris that the lake had swallowed up, there would be no time to gather everything that had been destroyed by the storm. Without all of the debris intact, the ball would probably not be big enough to plug the hole.

There were also problems with the stability of the debris ball. The townsfolk probably wouldn't have enough rope to secure all of the debris inside the ball, which would result in leaks and eventual breakdown of the blockage. The third problem would be the amount of wood needed to build a winch up to the sky. If all of the debris wood were used in the ball, there would be none left for the winch. No, she thought, any object that they used to block the sky would have to be a solid piece, and not require the use of any wood to stabilize it.

Merdona was a fairly large town, despite its remote perch on the mountain. The wood from the wreckage and the craftsmen's supply yards would be enough to build a winch. The only thing that remained to do was to find an object big enough to plug the hole. . .

"That's it," Genya cried, standing up, "We can use the whale to plug the hole in the sky!"

The large men in front of her spread out so that others could see her. Ox's brow darkened and creased.

He rumbled, "Genya, I told you not to come here."

Genya felt her face grow hot for a moment. The crowd was very quiet, but no one moved toward her. She cleared her throat, and continued.

"I. . . I know you told me not to come, but please, listen. Then if you want to, you can throw me out yourself. The whale has a broken fin, so he would be easy to catch. He's also big enough to plug the hole. He was barely thin enough to fit through when he fell out, and now he's gotten fatter from lazing around on the roof of the old inn and eating fish all day. All we need is a harness, a winch along the side of the sky scaffold, and lots of volunteers. As long as we keep him fed he'll keep plugging the hole."

As Genya spoke, more and more people in the crowd stopped what they were doing and paid attention. The tall men in front of her were the first to turn to Ox when she finished speaking.

"What do we do, Ox? Her idea is a good one, but you did tell her not to come here."

More people spoke out.

"I likes her plan!" Shouted Eustace.

"She's just copying my stratergem," said the old woman.

Ox stroked his beard. For several minutes, he let the crowd yell out their opinions while he stared intensely at Genya. In her outcast's corner she stood very still, waiting for the first pair of hands to seize on her.

Finally, Ox raised an arm.

"We'll design the needed equipment for the outlander's plan tonight, and in the morning we will start construction. As for Genya, she will stay at the inn during the construction, where she belongs," he said. "All in favour, say aye."

Genya almost fell over at the unanimity of the word 'aye' as it resounded throughout the hall. One of the large men in front of her took hold of her wrist.

"Well, you heard the Guild master, Miss. Let's go."

* * *

As Genya ran, she mouthed prayers punctuated by her own ragged breathing. Karlo, the man set to guard her at the inn, chased close behind. She had sworn to herself, on the night of the meeting, that she would stay out of the village's affairs from then on. Then pieces started to fall off of the sky scaffold.

She paused on the fourth landing of the scaffold to catch what breath was left in her after shimmying out of a privy window, stealing a large canvas satchel full of fish from the inn yard, and dashing all the way to the scaffold ahead of a large mob of angry townsfolk. The mob remained in the relative safety of the tents down below, yelling a mixture of taunts for her and encouragement for Karlo.

When Karlo reach the third landing, she decided to carry on. The boards underneath her began to shake. Up above the whale swung about in his rope harness and bellowed.

"OOOOOOOOOOOOON!"

Genya grasped a piece of railing on the stairs, only to have it tear away in her hand. She slipped on the soaked, smooth wood and, for a moment, found herself staring at the ground a hundred feet below. The sound of Karlo's shouts grew louder. Despite an oozing cut on her forearm Genya forced herself to look up and continue to climb.

After a few more flights of stairs, she felt her arms start to go numb, as though she were floating. The rain and the scaffold went double in her vision. The whale bellowed again, this time striking the side of the scaffold with his tail. One of the stairs from above jarred loose and struck Genya in the forehead. Everything became a blue-grey blur, but she heard Karlo on the landing just below her and knew she must press on. Step by step, she felt her way along with her feet and slowly her clarity of vision returned.

The whale dangled from the winch a hundred more feet up the stairs. The sight of him caused Genya to push her body harder, determined out outrun her guard. If they put her in jail for doing this, she thought, at least they'd be alive to do so. The water would not wait for them to build another scaffold. Shoving herself up the stairs one at a time, she looked upward to the place where she needed to go.

Just as she could see the whale's back over the top of the stairs, she felt a hand grab her ankle. Karlo held tight while she tried to struggle up the rest of the way. Her other foot slid out from underneath her and she tried to tuck it up to her chest to avoid his grasp. His features frowned out at her like wet leather draped over a saddle.

"You are endangering both of our lives, girl! Come back down quietly and after the plan is carried out you will go home," he pleaded.

Genya loosened her grip on the sack of fish on her back, causing a cascade of carp to pour over Karlo's head. The surprise caused his hand to slip just enough for her to wrench free, close the sack again and dash with what fish still remained to the edge of the sky scaffold. The whale caught sight of her and bellowed.

"OOOOOOOOOOOOON!" he said, flailing his tail. Wood groaned, letting Genya see the spaces in between the slats widen with every outward swing of the whale sling. A few paces behind her, a piece of flooring flew out of place with a hearty snap and plummeted through the hole it left behind. Shielding her eyes from the flying splinters and the rain, she assessed the distance between herself and the sling. The whale swung closer, reached an apex... and Genya jumped, her leg extended to close the gap.

Her right foot touched on a section of rope, but the weight of the sack of fish pulled her backward in a way that she had not anticipated. Her left hand scrabbled for a grip while she concentrated on keeping hold of the fish with her right. When she managed to grab on to a piece of netting, the barbs bit into her fingers. The whale's huge, sticky eye rolled over to look at her. His tail swung back and forth slowly, and he made a low grumbling sound.

"That's good," Genya panted, heaving the sack of fish over the side of the net, "Keep looking at me, whale. Looking won't break the scaffold"

She hooked her left foot into the net, and slowly inched her way toward the opening at the top. While she moved, she kept talking.

"That's it... just a few more steps and I'll be over. There we go, now I'm in the net with you. Don't panic, big guy." Genya soothed.

As soon as she was over the lip, she took up her sack and picked up a particularly fat fish. Reaching out over the whale's head and nose, she dangled it by the tail and let it wiggle in the wind. His beady eye followed it back and forth. He squeezed an airy sigh from his blow-hole. To Genya's delight, he opened his mouth, letting a shiny, triangular tongue speckled with bristles protrude out into the rain. His tail had stopped moving entirely in his concentration on the fish.

"Ah, I see that we have a compromise, Mr. Whale." She said, giving the fish a final wiggle. No sooner had it hit the whale's tongue than it was gone, sucked back into the giant's belly. Genya reached out, hand shaking, and patted him on the back.

Up above, a pair of burly men peered over the topmost tier of the scaffold. Genya recognized them as two of Ox's guildsmen. One of them called, "Get out of the sling and go with Karlo, there, missy. The whale is calm now."

Genya held up a fish for the guildsman to see.

"Sorry, I can't do that. It's the fish that are keeping him calm, and I have the fish." She called back.

First one guildsman, then the other disappeared behind the edge of the top deck. The scaffold crew flashed a lantern twice toward the ground, signalling their counterparts at the bottom to start the winch. The ropes creaked, the whale shifted its weight and then the whole sling continued upward.

The whale stuck out his tongue, making a quiet hooting noise. Genya pulled another fish from her sack and dropped it into his mouth.

As Genya traveled upward with the sling, the sound of rushing water grew louder. Stinging jets of cold rain sanded her skin. Rivulets ran down the spiral grooves of the ropes. What fish still remained intact and alive in her sack flapped their bodies almost in half to try and reach a larger body of water.

The men at the top of the scaffold remained safe by tying lengths of rope around their waists and between their legs and then attaching them to the vertical posts left behind from the smashing of the observation deck. They plodded around the edges of the platform because the pressure of the downpour in the middle would abrade their skin. Clothing whipped in the wind while hair remained plastered to their faces.

Ox waited for Genya and the whale. His team of six strong guildsmen stood in a line behind him holding ropes ended with self-closing metal hooks. Genya started to climb the side of the net to jump across, but Ox held up his hand.

"If you can't stay where I put you, then you can help where you're at," he yelled over the roar of the wind, "Secure the ropes as we toss them, and for sun's sake keep that beast calm."

The first rope came sailing through the air almost before Genya had a chance to nod. She reached up, caught the iron hook and clamped it onto the nearest support rope. Another guildsman tossed the next rope, but it fell just short of Genya's reach and struck the whale at the base of his tail. She nabbed the hook just as the whale's fluke knocked her backward into the crack between its body and the sling. As the whale thrashed, Genya struggled not to fall further down where she could be crushed by its weight. Her sack slipped down below the whale's belly. She inched along toward the second support rope and snapped it into place.

The third guildsman paused on the platform, holding his rope with the hook dangling down from his hand.

Genya hollered, "Just throw me the rope! I can handle this!"

Biting his lip in concentration the burly guildsman swung his rope around in a loop twice then let it fly. Genya caught it. As more ropes attached to the net, more guildsmen appeared from around the platform to pull them taut. By the time Genya secured all of the ropes, the whale was unable to move the net by shaking or flapping its tail. Thirty men held the net stable, with Ox in the middle directing them.

"Okay, Genya now hop the gap and find something to hold on to. We're going to swing this whale into its new home." He said, extending his arms to catch her.

She climbed up the side of the net, swaying a little in the wind at the edge. Squinting her eyes both against the rain and the urge to look down, Genya jumped across the gap to the platform.

Ox reached out over the edge to keep her from coming up short. He hauled her onto the platform with his sturdy arms set in a ring beneath her armpits. Before Genya could thank him he shoved her toward one of the vertical beams at the corners of the platform. The guildsmen were already heaving, their backs straining, pulling the whale towards the platform. When the sling tilted slightly, they let the ropes go, making the whole sling swing backward. The sling swung back toward the guildsmen, and they pulled harder to sharpen the arc.

The whale swung back and forth in its sling, higher and higher, until finally its tail touched the jet of water issuing from the hole in the sky.

"Ooooooon," the whale crooned, enjoying the sensation of the water on its skin. At the apex of the next swing it slipped from the harness up into the air where it traveled a bit further before slipping into the hole in the sky. The hole traveled up over its tail, covered its torso, wedged up over its front fins and then stopped abruptly at its neck. The whale wiggled once or twice then bellowed. It was most definitely stuck.

Down below on the platform, Genya wiped a drenched forelock away from her face. With the exception of a few drips, no more rain fell on the sky scaffold. The waves in the sky lost their foamy caps, smoothed and drifted away.

* * *

Genya sat at the bar of the Bull and Breeches, sipping a glass of the barkeep's finest blood red wine. As she sloshed a mouthful around in her cheeks a woman in a stained server's apron pushed by, dropping a platter of food in front of her.

On the platter were mashed potatoes, mixed vegetables and a ceramic pot filled with steaming fish chowder. She leaned back on her barstool. The new lake around Merdona shone with sky-fish, but the inns didn't just give fish away.

Genya addressed the waitress, leaning her elbow on the arm of her high legged chair.

"Doress, are fish really becoming so hard to get rid of that you're giving them away for free?" She asked, smiling.
Doress pointed to a table in the corner. "Compliments of the gentleman," she said.

The light of sunset streaming through the diamond-paned windows around him made Ox's shiny brown hair into a patchwork quilt of dappled orange. He lifted a tankard in Genya's direction with his head bowed.

Genya took her platter and headed for Ox's table.

"Thanks," she said to Doress, "It looks like he has an extra chair."

Doress chuckled once, pulled a cloth from her sash and scrubbed the section of bar Genya vacated.

Genya made eye contact and smiled while placing her platter on Ox's table. He tilted his head, reddening.

Once settled, Genya gathered some potatoes on her fork.

"I heard you're meeting with the mayor about the scaffold. It doesn't seem wise for you to be seen with me just now," she said.

Ox scratched the hairs on his forearm. Then he rubbed the side of his beard.

"The whale needs to be taken care of. It's been three days, and he's getting hungry," he grumbled.

Genya asked, "What does that have to do with me? I'm going back home. . . well, I'm not staying here, anyway."

Ox pressed his lips together, making the lower half of his face a solid mass of beard.

"The flood water isn't going anywhere. It will be tough for you to get out of town without a bridge."

Genya pulled her hair behind her ears with both hands, saying, "It shouldn't take too long for the Merdonan carpenters to finish a bridge if they all work together. There's more than enough wood in the winch."

"We want you to help, Genya," Ox said, taking a long swig from his tankard.

Genya stopped poking at her potatoes.

"Pardon me?"

"I mean it," Ox said, "We mean it. Stay in Merdona and you can work on the new bridge with us, and then the new observation deck for the sky scaffold."

Genya raised an eyebrow.

Ox explained, "The mayor can't light the pyres when the whale is so close. I said before that someone needs to feed him. The sky scaffold has to stay or else he'll get skinny and open up the hole again."

"If I stay here and feed the whale, I get to name him," Genya said, holding out her left hand over the table.

Ox took her hand and slapped his other hand over top in the craftsmen's greeting.

"You have a deal. Welcome to the Guild, Genya."

Genya smiled.

"So, what's his name?" Ox asked.

Genya giggled, saying, "I named him right after he fell from the sky. He's Mr. Oon. M'oon for short."

Ox returned Genya's smile.

"That's perfect," he said.

Thank You For Reading With Pop Seagull Publishing!

If you enjoyed this book, then you'll love our first novel...

Flood Waters Rising

An epic tale of love, loyalty and war among an alien race.

Coming July 2011!

For exclusive content, updates and fun, connect with us online at:

Twitter: @PopSeagullPub
Website: http://www.popseagullpublishing.com
Blog: http://popseagullpublishing.wordpress.com/
Smashwords: http://www.smashwords.com/profile/view/popseagullpublishing

About the Author

Elizabeth Hirst lives in Oakville, Ontario, Canada with her fiance, her best friend, five fish and a lizard named Creep. She has published work in Alien Skin Magazine (http://www.alienskinmag.com/) the Mystic Signals 3 Anthology (http://www.loreleisignal.com) and is a former creative writer for Hitgrab Inc, creators of the MouseHunt and Levynlight Facebook apps. http://www.hitgrab.com/. In addition to her efforts as a writer and publisher, Elizabeth is training to be a professional animator at Sheridan College.

Photo by Sheena Callighen, 2010

Made in the USA
Charleston, SC
08 February 2013